A COWGIRL'S TRAIL

ANNETTE ILOWIECKI

Based on true events
from my earlier "cowgirl years"
connect with me on FB Page
"Don't They Just Set You To Dreaming?"

*To everyone who wanted to be a
"cowboy when they grew up"
And have their very own cow pony.
Enjoy the ride.*

CONTENTS

A COWGIRL'S TRAIL

About two weeks after Carla Johnson graduated from high school, she announced to her astonished parents, "Mom, Dad, I'm joining the Marine Corps Reserves. "

"You know honey, the Air Force is an easier branch to pursue. I've heard they give women who want to be Marines a tough time. Not that you couldn't handle it, but the Air Force is more accepting of women in military roles. I know it's wrong for people to discriminate like that but it's just how it is. So, why the Marines?"

"Dad, ever since I read about Sgt. Reckless, I wanted to experience some of her world. She served our country with her band of brothers in the Korean War. I appreciate your concerns, but I figure I couldn't do anything less than a horse. She was a Marine and I just have to be one too."

"I know out of all the horse stories you've read, Sgt. Reckless grabbed your heart. She inspired you. But what about being a cowgirl? You've put a lot of effort into getting experience working with horses. I wouldn't want all that to go to waste."

"Mom, I don't know how all this is going to work out. But the reserves are one weekend a month and two weeks a year, so there's room for being a cowgirl in there somewhere."

"Unless you get deployed."

"That's the bottom line of what we sign up for Dad, if that happens I'll be ready to go."

~

ON THE BUS ride to Paris Island, Carla thought back to all of her childhood prayers which always went along these lines: "Dear God, Please make me a Cowboy when I grow up. Bless Mom, Dad and all the cattle on the ranch, well you know, I mean the cows on the farm. Bless Grandma and Grandpa, well you know, the whole family. And God "Flash" is just imaginary, but could you please, somehow bring me a real live cow pony of my own?" "Well God, you might be tired of hearing this request, just like mom gets tired of hearing my **"Gunfighter Legends and Trail Songs"** record album, so I'll just say "Good Night God and Thanks for listening."

Carla smiled at the memory. Then felt inclined to continue the conversation, "Well God, I still don't have my 'very own cow pony' and now here I am on a bus to Paris Island, in the Marine Corps. But Sgt. Reckless never became the race horse that she was bred for, and she ended up serving a cause way bigger then herself. I hope I'm on the right trail God, I think I am. I'd still like to have my very own cow pony and be a "cowboy" when I grow up. But it's been a pretty good trail so far...

"Like the summer my best friend Amanda and I, worked at the **J Bar J** Ranch, a small 40 acre horse farm, in exchange for learning everything John and Julie could teach us about horses."

"Handling poop scoopers, latigos, bridles, saddles, harnesses, became second nature. Sitting a horse at walk, trot, canter and letting go of that saddle horn while flying along at full gallop became as easy to me as sleeping in my boots. A practice I only got away with for one night, then Mom talked me out of it." Carla laughed to herself at that memory.

"Even after school started, we were there on weekends. We became horse show grooms to their Half-Arabian mare "Dream Girl". Who would have thought we'd get to take off school and go to the U.S. National Arabian Horse Show, in Louisville Kentucky. "Dream Girl" placed National Reserve Champion. We were there. We served that fiery, talented horse and we helped make that happen. Thanks God for this good trail you've led me on so far. Dear Lord, help me ride through this next one, I really have no idea what I've just sign up for."

THE BUS AIR BRAKES SQUEECHED. A Marine Drill Instructor stepped on the bus.

"What are you jokers doing on my bus? I need everyone right now, put your heads up, with all eye balls on me and YELL, 'Mam! Yes Mam!' This is the way you will answer any drill instructor who asks you a question? Is that understood?"

"Mam! Yes Mam!"

"I can't hear you! Get those baby binkies out of your mouths and answer me."

"Mam! Yes Mam!"

"Now when I tell you, you will all stand up, you will get off my bus, you will stand on the yellow foot prints on the deck! You will then wait for further instructions! Is that understood?"

"Mam! Yes mam!"

"Now Get **OFF MY BUS!**"

Boot Camp at Paris Island, South Carolina was more difficult then Carla could have imagined. But if the brave mare Reckless could be a Marine, then so could Carla. When she finally earned that title, with mom and dad in attendance at the ceremony, all she could think to say was "Thank you God for getting me through this."

OF ALL THE places to get shipped, Carla arrived at Camp Pendleton for Field Wireman MOS training. While standing in a line being "welcomed aboard" her thoughts drifted, "Sergeant Reckless lived the last

14 years of her life here after serving in the war. She was buried with full military honors in 1968. I wish I could walk the pasture where she walked. I was born in 1966. We were alive at the same time for 2 years. How I wish I could have met her, combed her mane, hugged her neck and gave her a salute..."

"Private Johnson! Did you hear me the 1st time? I said your barracks assignment is with Sanchez. You got 15 minutes to double-time it over there, check in, and be in time for Chow! I'm sure they aren't serving steak and lobster tonight to welcome you to Pendleton, but you should find something to choke down. I hope you pay better attention when you start climbing poles!"

"Yes sir! Captain, thank you, we are going now! Sir."

"Ohhhh no that was a bad 1st impression, I'm day dreaming about my horse hero and I have no idea, what the check in procedure is." Carla quietly chided herself as her and Sanchez "double-timed it" to the barracks.

"Okay who do we have here? You must be Privates' Johnson and Sanchez. You're the only two left on the list who haven't checked in yet.

All right Privates, your dorm room is 302, the elevator is down the hall to the right or you can be real Marines and double-time it up the stairs."

The sergeant continued, "I'd catch some chow first though, they'll stop serving at 1830 hours. Here's your MOS schedule and orders, keep track of these papers. They won't issue you another copy! Pick up a map at the end of this table. I'd suggest you highlight the locations of your MOS classes and know how to get there ahead of time. Don't show up late! Okay, You're good to go. Welcome Aboard Camp Pendleton Privates."

"Thank you, Sergeant."

~

CHICKEN PATTY ON A BUN, dried up mashed potatoes and buttered corn was their welcoming meal to Camp Pendleton. "Did you read this,

Sanchez? They ship us out here in a hurry, and now MOS School doesn't start for 3 weeks."

"Typical military, hurry up and wait. I guess we get to police the grounds for three weeks, or maybe work in the Chow Hall? I'm sure they'll find something for us to do."

"Oh no! Not the Chow Hall, or policing the grounds! I didn't get all the way out here this close to where Sgt. Reckless lived and not go there. I'm not waiting for an assignment, I'm going to request to work at the Stables!"

"Well, that sounds like a great idea for a horse loving Marine, you go for it, Private Cowgirl. Good luck making **that** request to the Captain!" "I'm going to "double-time it" to his office 1st thing in the morning!"

"PRIVATE, Johnson. I hope you're done with your daydreaming and are better focused now."

"I am Sir"

"So you and Sanchez got checked in all right?"

"We did Sir."

"So what brings you to my office, Private?"

"I have three weeks of down time before Wireman School starts. I would like to request to work at the stables during that time Sir."

"Private Johnson, I can't believe what you're asking me, we usually send Marines to work at the stables for punishment, and you want to go there?"

"Yes sir" I have experience with horses. I believe I could be an asset to them sir."

"You might end up shoveling horse manure and bucking hay bales for 3 weeks Private. Are you prepared to do that?"

"If that's what they assign me to, "yes sir."

"They might not take kindly to a Female Marine barging into their territory."

"I will earn their respect, just like Sergeant Reckless did sir"

"I appreciate that sentiment, Private. Reckless was a true war hero. I don't have anything better to do with your class for the next three weeks except assign you all to policing the grounds. This is what I'll do. I'm granting you permission to give this a try. But mind you, Gunnery Sergeant Woods is an old school, hard-ass Marine. He's in charge of the stables and knows what's going to work over there. Go see him 1st thing in the morning. If he approves this deal, you are good to go. If things don't work out, report back to me at 1300 hours."

"Yes sir! Thank you sir!"

"FINALLY, I'm going to see the last home of Sergeant Reckless." Carla thought to herself on her way back to the barracks. "I wonder if Gunny Woods is going to go for this. "Well, Ooh Rah Marine Corps, just got to ride this trail and see where it goes. I'll make my introduction to old "hard-ass" Gunny and hope for the best."

The next morning Carla made her introduction to Gunny Woods at 0900 hours. "All right Pvt. Johnson, you're telling me you have some horse experience. I assume you also **think that you know** how to ride. So this is what I'll do."

Then like right out of a John Wayne movie, Gunnery Sergeant Woods pointed to a horse in the corral. "See that horse down there, that red mare with the long white blaze?"

"I see her Gunny."

"Her name is Jill Marine. This is your lucky day. It's been over a week since she decided to come in. I guess she wanted that scoop of grain bad enough today to be confined for a while. Well, **if** you can throw a saddle on her and ride her, **then** you can work here. Just ask any of the boys to show you where her tack is."

Carla took a deep breath and walked to the tack shed. She asked one of "the boys" where to find Jill's. He looked at her with astonishment, "Are you going to ride her? "

"That's the plan."

"That horse hasn't been ridden in over a year."

"She's going to be ridden today."

"**NONE of us** ride Jill, we don't even bring her into the stalls: she just runs wild around the pasture all day, comes in the corral with the others only if she wants to."

The thought crossed her mind, "WHAT in the WORLD have you got yourself into?" But she quickly pushed it out. "Carla you rode Amber, that powerful little barrel racing, Quarter Horse at the **J Bar J**. She was as fiery as they come. Surely this 'Jill horse' is no more difficult. Show confidence Johnson, no matter what, ACT LIKE riding a horse that 'Runs wild in the pasture all day' is what you were born to do."

"Ok, her tack is over there in the corner,"

"Thanks."

While Carla dusted off the saddle, checked stirrup lengths and brushed cobwebs off the saddle blanket, she heard chatter in the background.

"Hey Dan, go fetch Gus and Brent, tell 'em to high-tail it down here and come watch the show. That Field Wiremen Broad, thinks she's going to ride Jill."

"How much you want to bet she can't?" Dan Asked.

"I'm keeping my money on Jill." Travis said.

"Yep, I'm with you Travis." Dan answered as he jogged out of the tack shed to fetch Gus and Brent.

"Focus Johnson, Carla told herself. "It's only you and Jill now. Watch her every move; be prepared for anything, a successful ride is the only acceptable outcome."

Carla carried Jill's tack into the corral. She set the saddle up on its horn, and draped the saddle blanket and bridle on it. She was vaguely aware of the four Marine Cowboys, leaned up against the fence rail, who had come to "watch the show".

"Boys the rodeo is about to begin." Travis laughed.

"Who is this gal anyway?" Gus asked.

Travis shrugged his wide shoulders, "She ain't no Texan—I can tell you that. Just some poor misguided Broad Ass Marine."

"Her ass ain't broad enough to sit in Jill's saddle," Gus countered as he spit chewing tobacco juice in the dust right beside Travis's cowboy boot.

For what seemed like hours, but was probably only minutes, Carla spoke softly to Jill, "Easy there, girl, whoa now, stand easy, let's show these yahoo's how to ride a horse."

"She's shore gonna' eat gravel today!" Brent added.

"She made it through boot camp, I'll give her that but boot camp is different than ridin' one of our Camp Pendleton wild ones." Dan said with a chuckle.

Jill allowed Carla to approach, reach under her tangled mane and rub her neck. The mare shuddered and tossed her head. "I want to trust you, but not sure I can," her cautious movements spoke.

Travis shook his head at the others. "I overheard her tell Gunny she's from a dairy farm. Milk cows boys, MILK cows! Are the slowest, tamest, biggest ugliest, lumbering critters there is. "Gettin' milk out of a cow and riding a horse like Jill, two different things boys, two different things."

"We've got work to do here, don't need no wanna'-be cowgirl to wet nurse like a new born calf. " Brent scoffed.

"You got that right. All she'll be is a heap of trouble. No Yankee Milk Maids here!" Dan said as he ground a cigarette butt into the dust with the toe of his cowboy boot.

Carla held out a grooming brush, allowing Jill to sniff it, to press her soft nose against it. She shied away and stepped sideways from every other brush stroke. She stood still for one, seeming to enjoy its scratchy feel then shied away from the next. Carla moved with her. They continued this dance around in circles until the shy mare stood still.

"Boys I got twenty bucks that says she won't last 3 minutes on that horse!" Travis pulled the bill out of his wallet and looked each wrangler in the eyes as they shook their heads.

"I'll take that bet."

"Ahhh Gunny you just have a soft spot for the underdog." Travis replied.

"Maybe, we'll see." Gunny answered.

"Gunny I've got $20, more that says Jill's going to win this round." Dan said.

"Anyone else boys?"

"Yep, we're all in Gunny" Brent and Gus chimed in.

"Yeah like no pressure," Carla thought to herself, "leave it to a bunch of Cowboy Marines to turn this into a betting match."

Even though they were all Marines, Carla was thankful that civilian dress was allowed at the stables. Her cowboy boots, blue jeans, Semper Fi t-shirt and Marine Corps baseball cap afforded some relief from the September California sun. She couldn't have imagined doing this in Cammie's and combat boots. There was some sense to the military.

"Well girl they'll respect us or despise us, let those chips fall where they may. We're going to have a successful ride today."

Like a lion stalking its prey, the "what ifs" attempted to sneak into her mind. "What if she throws me? What if she bucks harder than I've ever rode before? What if. .. No time for questions Johnson, just calm, confident action."

She had to maintain a show of confidence for Jill, and for those yahoo's leaning on the fence rail. Carla gently slipped a lead rope around Jill's neck, the mare continued to shy away. Carla applied gentle pulls on the rope cuing her to stand still.

"Ok girl stand easy and let's get your bridle on. Carla draped her right arm over the top of Jill's head, holding the bridle in place while coaxing her to accept the bit. The horse threw her head up and lifted Carla off her feet.

This was exactly how John, back at the **J Bar J** had taught her to bridle a horse. "Don't let go, even if they throw their head up and lift you off your feet. They'll get tired of you hanging there, and put you back down."

Carla read the mare's thoughts. "Like you've been nice and all up to this point, but BIT and BRIDLE? NO WAY NOT DOING IT!" After Carla's feet were on the ground again, and that bridle was still on Jill's head, the mare seemed to be saying, "Ok, I see that you're persistent about this, so I'll let you put that hard metal thing in my mouth."

"That's right, good girl, good horse. Now that's not so bad is it?"

Jill's ears turned to and fro catching the sound of Carla's voice. The mare watched Carla's every move as she stepped away, picked up the blanket and saddle. Jill tossed her head and jumped sideways. Carla continued to approach slow and easy while speaking softly.

Another sideways jump. Carla kept speaking quietly and slowly placed the saddle blanket on her back with her left hand while holding the saddle by its horn and letting it hang against her right leg.

"Ok girl, I know it's been awhile since you wore all this stuff, but it's okay, we're going to be the best of friends." She swung the saddle up, and gently set it on her back.

Jill replied. Stomping and pawing her front hooves, shaking her head, even a little crow hopping. Carla kept hold of the saddle and moved with the mare until she stood still.

Carla laughed softly and stroked her neck. With more crow hops, and pawing up dust, Jill finally accepted tightening the girth strap. Now it was time for the mare to accept Carla.

"Jill, we're going to have a nice smooth ride. We are going to show these jokers what a great horse you are." Carla spoke with gentle yet firm authority.

The mare cocked her ear back. "Good sign she's listening to my voice," Carla thought. I have her attention. " Carla gathered up a handful of red mane while firmly grasping the reins. She placed her left foot in the stirrup and applied pressure.

Jill bowed her head and jumped sideways. Carla hopped along with her. When she stopped Carla took her foot out of the stirrup, stood beside her until she was calm.

"We're going to have a calm ride and show these Smart Alec's how great you are." While the mare was listening, Carla regained her hold onto mane and reins, placed her foot back in the stirrup, and swung into the saddle.

Jill stood still for a moment, Carla clicked to her and gently nudged with her heels, sending a message that as the leader of the herd, Carla was directing the mare's next move.

Jill exploded forward, tossed her head, kicked up her back feet, all at the same time. Carla hung onto the saddle horn with her right hand and pulled Jill's head to her side with the reins. The mare had no choice but to go in circles. She finally got tired of this and stood still. Carla stroked her neck, "Jill you are a great horse."

They moved through a few walk, trot and canters until she smoothed out her strides.

"Pay up Boys! This Greenhorn might not be so green heh? Take one last look at your money before you kiss it good bye!"

"Well Gunny, you sure called this one right. We're eating humble pie for supper tonight." Travis said while looking down at his boots.

"Yep, I'll make sure they serve it up at the Chow Hall!" Gunny replied.

"How in the HELL did she just do that?" Brent Emphasized his question with a tobacco juice spit as they all shook their heads.

"Maybe her ass is broad enough to sit in Jill's saddle," Gus muttered.

"It's time to saddle up boys, take a couple hours and show this greenhorn girl and her wild horse around the trails."

"We're on it Gunny" Travis replied. They all nodded and went to get their horses.

"Well Pvt. Johnson, I guess you do know something about horses, you've got yourself a job and a guide horse."

"Thank you, Gunnery Sargent Woods."

"I think we'll get along fine, she's a dandy.'

"Yep, one of our best."

FOR THE NEXT THREE WEEKS, every weekend and possible evening during

Field Wireman School, Jill and Carla led riders over Camp Pendleton's back country trails. "These are the same trails that Sergeant Reckless walked, these are the same pastures where she grazed. She had her colts here, 'Fearless', 'Dauntless', and 'Chesty' and one filly who died before she was named. How is it possible that I've come to this place? Living my 'cowboy dream', with more horses then I have time to ride?"

"Thank you God for answering my prayer. You haven't sent me my very own cow pony, but here I am, at least on evenings and weekends, "being a cowboy when I grow up." It's been a pretty good trail so far."

Graduating from Field Wireman School marked the end of a dream fulfilled. With tears in her eyes, Carla hugged Jill's neck and said good bye to her beloved "wild horse."

"Johnson, I guess this is the end of the trail for us. It's "shore" been a pleasure wrangling horses with ya. We're all sorry to see you go.

Semper Fi Marine." Travis said in his Texas drawl.

"Thanks Travis, Gus, Dan, Brent, you guys are the best crew of Marine Cowboys I've ever known. I'll always remember these trails we rode together."

CARLA STOOD in front of Sgt. Reckless' grave marker.

In Memory of
"RECKLESS",
Pride of The Marines
KOREA,
July 1949-May 1968

"WELL SGT. RECKLESS, I've stepped into your world. I became a Marine. It's been one heck of a ride so far. Thanks for your inspiration. Thanks for your service to our country. I'm sure God has a special place for you in heaven. I look forward to seeing you there. Until then Comrade, All is Well, Safely Rest. God is Nigh." Against the scenery of that back-country California landscape, Carla stood at attention and rendered her best Marine Corps salute.

ABOUT A YEAR LATER, Carla's Marine Corps unit shipped out to Fort Carson, Colorado for their annual two week training. She was thrilled to have another all-expense paid trip to a landscape where cowboys ride.

During one day of liberty, she and a couple buddies went looking for something to do. "Why don't we find a ranch and go for a trail ride?" Carla suggested.

"Not surprised that suggestion is coming from our horse crazy Jar Head, but it sounds like fun. Let's give it a shot." During their two hour ride through some of the most breath taking scenery Carla had ever been in, she asked the guide if the Ranch was hiring.

"It turns out that Mr. Clayton, our Ranch Foreman is looking for one more guide for the season."

Carla was hired on a handshake with a disclaimer. Mr. Clayton explained, "Getting off for drill once a month is easy, there's a reserve unit in Denver that your Captain should be able to get you connected with. But you told me you know how to handle horses, if I see that you don't know what you're doing, I'm going to send you packing right back home."

"Fair enough. Mr. Clayton, Thank you."

CARLA COMPLETED her drill at Fort Carson and flew home with her unit. Then over a weekend, with faith in God as her trail guide, she packed up her Firebird and drove to Silverthorne, Colorado.

She arrived with $5.00 cash in her pocket and stepped into her dream job AGAIN! This time riding horses, through the Rocky Mountains at the Eagle Ridge Ranch.

She had been on the job about 2 weeks, the sky was rumbling, wranglers were scrambling to un-tack horses, a gusty wind chilled off the hot summer air, dark clouds began to spit out cold drops.

"Let's get these horses moving' we need one wrangler up!" Mr. Clayton yelled.

The ultimate "you're one of us now" things to do was to be "THAT" wrangler. They were always the last one to leave, with 1 more horse to un-tack, and the barn to lock up. Even so it was a highly coveted position except today- NO ONE- volunteered for it, No One that is except Carla.

With a little faith, and just knowing she had to do this in this moment, "I got it" she yelled.

"Here's your mount" wrangler Tammy held onto Rat's lead rope as Carla took a deep breath and climbed aboard. Rat, with the raggedy "rat" tail, was a retired rodeo contesting horse.

The thrill of riding this talented, athletic equine, was the reason ALL the wranglers usually clamored to do this, but today everyone just wanted to go home.

The storm transferred its nervous energy to the horses. Rat's ears were pointed forward, every muscle coiled tight, ready to spring. Rat and Carla herded this skittery bunch of horse flesh out of the corral, up the gravel road a ways, and into the night pasture.

The lead horses reached the gate and entered the pasture, It looked like the rest of them would follow. Rat trotted easily now alongside the stragglers.

Suddenly a flash of lighting cracked open the sky. Just like on cue, three horses veered away from the herd; they kicked up their heels, stretched out their necks, and challenged the storm to outrun them.

In one fluid motion, Rat spun on his heels and JUMPED into full gallop. At the same time, Carla grabbed the saddle horn and prayed "GOD HELP!" to stay seated during this rocket launch. She leaned forward, gave her horse full reign and yelled, "Let's get "em Rat!"

Mud, gravel, cold rain, pelted her face, thunder roared, lightning flashed. They galloped through the storm. Gained ground, got closer, closer still.

Then they pulled slightly ahead of the renegades, giving them just enough edge, with Rats superior speed and his rodeo contesting skills, they headed off and stopped those three horses.

They turned them towards the fence and trotted them back to the gate. The wranglers cheered, Tammy handed Carla her mud covered hat. In that moment Carla KNEW she was one of them now.

Carla leaned forward from the saddle and hugged Rat's neck. "Thanks boy, you are a GREAT horse."

"And God, thank you for answering my prayer. Thank you for bringing me to this place. Here I am again being a "cowboy when I grow up, and You still haven't brought me my very own cow pony - but maybe this is the next best thing."

AFTER 3 MONTHS of guiding tourists over the same trails, through the same meadows and forests, six hours a day, Carla was ready for a change. She never dreamed riding horses through beautiful mountain scenery could actually become, well, kind of boring, but in a pleasant kind of way. She wanted to ride somewhere she'd never ridden before, without being responsible for a line of tourists behind her on horseback.

"Hold up there, Carla,"

"Yes Mr. Clayton?"

"We have two hunters that Luke is packing up the mountain tomorrow. He's going to need an extra hand to lead a pack horse." I know you've wanted to get experience with that, considered yourself volunteered for the job."

"Thank you, Mr. Clayton, I appreciate this opportunity."

The hunter's camp was located at 11,000 foot elevation on Red Mountain. This was a chance to get a crash course in tracking and reading sign in wild country. The next morning Carla met Luke at the barn.

"Saddle up Ace it will be good training for him, he needs experience leading a pack horse."

"So do I." Carla said.

"Well you're gonna' get some today! Just be mindful of going between trees and through narrow gaps. Watch behind ya and be sure the lead rope doesn't get hung up. Be ready to give your pack horse some help, if he gets off balance jumping over logs, across creeks and things." Scout has done a lot of packin' so he'll help you both figure it out."

"Thanks Luke, I'm sure we are in for an adventure today."

"Yep it always is with this ride. It's been a year since I packed anyone up there."

Carla tacked up the riding horses, while Luke loaded the packs on Starlight, and Scout.

"Here ya go sir, his name is Casbar Twist, I think we got the stirrups adjusted for you.

"Thanks, just call me Ken." Carla held Casbar while "Ken" mounted up. Then she assisted the other hunter with "Major."

THE GORE-RANGE TRAIL leading away from the Ranch was wide, smooth, riding. But the trail leading up to the hunter's camp was a challenge even for Luke to follow. They crept up the mountain through turnarounds, creek crossings, log jumpings, and narrow passages.

"I'm riding through some more of your world, Sgt. Reckless," Carla said to herself. "Except we're not packing ammunition to the front lines under heavy artillery fire so we got this. Ace and Scout, let's make Sgt. Reckless proud."

About 4 hours later, Carla, Ace and Scout breathed a sigh of relief at the sight of the hunter's camp. While checking their supplies, they discovered the cooking gear didn't get packed. Luke told them that someone would "run it up to them tomorrow."

Carla smiled to herself hearing that phrase, and thought "like it'll be no problem just "running back up this mountain."

Luke handed Scout and Major's lead ropes to Carla. He led Casbar Twist and Starlight. The trek back down the mountain, while still challenging, was easier.

The Ranch was a welcome sight. All the horses happily chomped their oats and enjoyed a good rub down before being turned out to the night pasture.

"Thanks God for a great day, and the crash course in pack horse training. That was a real cowboy adventure."

THE NEXT DAY, Carla was the only person available to take the cooking gear back up the mountain. She didn't need a pack horse for this trip, so she saddled up Mama Pepper. This sturdy, dappled gray Appaloosa mare had become Carla's favorite guide horse at Eagle Ridge.

She continually cocked her ears to listen to Carla's voice. Carla trusted Mama's twelve years' experience of surviving the harshness of the mountains. She knew how to step over steep rocky trails and seek firm ground through swampy marshlands. She saved her running for smooth open places.

Carla's "Resistal" cowboy hat, oilskin jacket and leather chaps protected her from weather and scraping branches. Her water canteen was in easy reach tied in front of her saddle. What more could Carla possibly need to find a hunter's camp on top of Red Mountain?

"Are you sure you can find the camp?" Luke asked.

"Yep no problem, I was just there yesterday, how hard can it be?"

When they crossed the third creek, Carla pulled up. Was she supposed to look for the trail head after the third creek crossing? Or after the fourth?

"Well Mama, after we get to the other side, I'll remember if we were there yesterday or not, and we can always come back. Right?" Mama balked. The creek was less than fifteen feet wide and not over a foot deep.

"Come on, Mama, step easy." The mare braced her front feet to protest a nudge from Carla's boot. Let's go!" Carla commanded. Mama whinnied and tossed her head but gingerly placed one hoof on the creek bottom. About four steps later, her front legs disappeared. Her body heaved as she was sucked chest deep into a pool of thick brown mud.

The little horse lunged forward, straining for stable footing. The saddle lurched as she scrambled and tried to swim through the gooey muck. "God, Help!"

Carla gave her horse full rein to have free use of her head. Beyond that there was nothing more Carla knew to do. She hung on and prayed that her weight wouldn't cause them to sink deeper. When Mama's knees surfaced, her hooves found solid ground.

"Oh thank you, God,"

Carla slid from Mama Pepper's back and hugged her neck. Thankfully there were no scratches or any sign of injury to the sturdy mountain horse.

"I'm so sorry. You knew this crossing was wrong and you were trying to tell me. Why didn't I listen?"

"Can you get us back across?" Mama pranced and shook her head. She picked her way downstream where the creek bed was firm and the water shallow.

"You had every reason to buck me off and leave me on this mountain, yet you didn't give up on me. You just carried me back to safety without a single 'I told you so'. You forgave me for my know-it-all attitude. Kind of just like God does. Okay faithful little guide horse, from now on, I'm listening to you."

"Mama, look! Those three gray tree stumps in a triangle leaning in towards each other that Luke told us to look for! Ya-Hoo! We're on the right trail now. There's our hoof prints from yesterday. "The trail merged into a rocky surface and the hoof prints became harder to follow. Finally they vanished.

"Hold up there Pepper." Luke's last minute advice surfaced in Carla's mind. "If you lose the trail, stop, look and think. Don't go anywhere until you see sign to follow. Your own hoof prints from backtracking can be confusing."

"Six horses at four hoofs apiece. Surely I should be able to spot at least one of 24 hoof prints from yesterday's ride. " Carla thought.

"Why hadn't I paid closer attention to landmarks and trail signs?" Carla chided herself. "What do you do after stopping, looking and thinking?"

"Ok God, which way do we go from here? "Only mountain silence answered.

"Ok, this is your way of giving me a chance to use the intelligence and instincts you gave me, to listen to that still small voice right? "She followed her first hunch and rode past a big rock to the left.

"Mama, look, there's a hoof print. Hey, there's a whole bunch of them."

More tracks. Piles of horse manure. Unusually shaped trees she had seen before. Each new "sign" added a notch to Carla's self-confidence.

"Thanks God, just help us keep following you."

THEY WERE MAKING STEADY PROGRESS. Then it began to snow. Within minutes, tons of swirling white flakes surrounded them. Visibility dropped to about 3 feet in every direction. "Well there goes the hoofprints. Ok little horse, what's the best thing to do in a Colorado snow storm when your half way up a mountain?"

They settled in under a cave-like shelter beneath some overhanging tree branches, just large enough for a horse and rider. Carla's only plan was to outlast the storm and pray the hunters did not mistake them for an Elk.

About twenty minutes later (but what seemed like hours) the snow stopped. A blanket of white covered the ground. "Ok girl, let's finish this mission. Sargent Reckless wouldn't give up and neither will we."

To Carla, there were only two directions. One was up; the other down. Since they hadn't found it yet, the hunter's camp had to be up. They began to zigzag their way up the mountain.

"Hello! At camp! Any one up here?" She shouted periodically. Finally, a man's voice called back.

"Thank you Jesus! We found them Mama!" The camp was nothing more than a small sparsely furnished lean-to providing just enough shelter to get out of severe weather.

"Pull up a rock by the fire. Have a beer and here's a sandwich," the hunters offered.

"Thanks," Carla gratefully accepted. A slice of bologna on bread washed down with beer never tasted so good.

"I've got your cooking gear in the pack. We're burning daylight, so we gotta get going. We'll be back up to pack ya' down on Friday."

"Okay mountain horse, I'm sure you know the way back to your oats.

Take us home, Mama Pepper." Carla looped the reins around the saddle horn and trusted herself to her horse. She dodged branches while her sturdy, wonderful, little gray Appaloosa nosed her way between trees, across creeks, over rocks and through narrow passage ways, until they reached the North-South Gore Range Trail.

No mistaking the way now. The sturdy little mountain horse broke into a canter over smooth, firm familiar ground. She whinnied, tossed her head, and shifted into a gallop at first glimpse of the ranch. Carla leaned over her neck, gave her full reign and yelled, "Yee Haw! Let's go home, little horse!"

Chilled October air settled in while dusk gave way to nightfall when they reached the corral. Carla "walked Mama out", gave her a thorough brushing and extra scoop of oats. "Always take care of your horse first, just like the real cowboys do," is an instruction Carla followed from childhood with her imaginary cow pony "Flash" to every horse under her care since.

As she led Mama Pepper out to the night pasture, Mama's ears turned to catch Carla's voice. "Well God that was another grand cowboy adventure. Thank you for getting us down off that mountain! You still haven't sent me my very own cow pony, but you sure have given me a lot of great horses to ride. It's been a pretty good trail so far. I'm going to keep trusting you to do what's best for me."

> *"Thank you God for bringing me to this place.*
> *And Thanks God for being*
> ***Always Faithful.***
> *Just like Sgt. Reckless.*
> *Just like a trusted mountain horse.*
> *Just like a Marine.*
> ***Semper Fi."***

ABOUT THE AUTHOR

Annette Ilowiecki lives on the shores of Stone Lake in Middlebury, Indiana. She belongs to **"The Stormy Night Writers Society"** a group of creative individuals who encourage and inspire each other to pursue their writing talents.

Connect with Annette on FB Page
Don't They Just Set You To Dreaming?

ALSO BY ANNETTE ILOWIECKI

Another book from Pony Books Plus, Inc.

Co-authored by Annette Ilowiecki and Peg Cook

"Don't They Just Set You To Dreaming?"

A story-poem that became a song.

It retells the legend with full color photos how the Chincoteague Wild Ponies
came to claim Assateague Island as their homeland.

Available at:

Sundial Books

https://www.book2look.com/book/hNcdwOqERT

Bluecrab Treasures Gift Shop

Chincoteague Pony Centre Gift Shop

(Find them on Face Book)